The Story of the Squatch

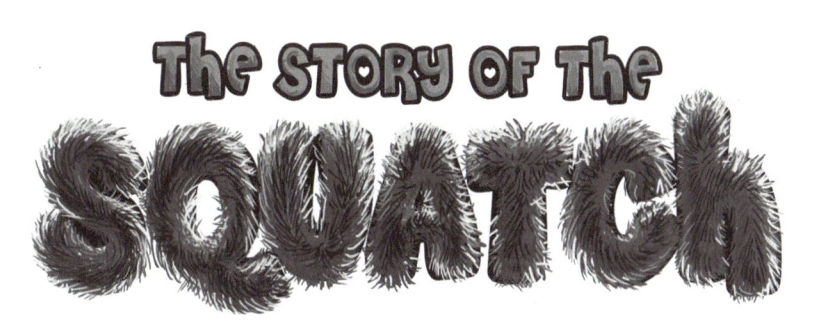

Be Kind.
Be Adventurous.

Written by **Jeremy Cross**
Illustrated by Kathrine Gutkovskiy

Copyright © 2021 by Jeremy Cross

All rights reserved. This book or any portion thereof may not be reproduced or used in any manner whatsoever without the express written permission of the publisher except for the use of brief quotations in a book review.

ISBN: 978-0-578-89254-2

CrossLab Publishing

Contact: theStoryoftheSquatch@gmail.com
Website: www.TheStoryOfTheSquatch.com

To my Mom, my Dad & my Brother,
for always letting me be as *weird* as I needed to be.

The forest is filled with creatures of all types and sizes. Many of them you have heard of. Some of them are a little less familiar. This is a story about one that you may not know…

High in the mountains lives a rare being, one that few humans have ever laid eyes upon…

The Squatch!

~~Sasquatch~~ ~~Bigfoot~~

Now, who is '**the Squatch**', you ask? Well, maybe you have heard of a being called "Sasquatch", "Bigfoot" or "Yeti". He is not they, and they are not him.

The Squatch in our story is actually a lot like you and me: He lives with his family. Dessert is his favorite meal. And he loves going on adventures.

In some ways though, the Squatch is **VERY** different from you and me: Instead of a house, he lives in a cave. Instead of a market, he gathers his food from the forest. And maybe you noticed, he is **COVERED** in fur from head to toe!

Now, because of where he lives, the Squatch has never actually seen a human before. And that's how it is supposed to be. Or so he was taught.

When the Squatch was very young, his parents told him always to **KEEP AWAY FROM HUMANS**. Humans and Squatch just do not mix, they said. His Grandpa even told him of times when humans cleared an **ENTIRE** forest just to build a super store!

Even after all of the stories, the Squatch often thought, "**ALL** humans can't be bad." And one day, he hoped to meet one. Maybe they could even be friends.

The Squatch had never left his forest, but he knew the world was a **BIG** place. And there were **BILLIONS** of humans. Surely at least **ONE** of them had to be nice…

One morning, the Squatch set out to pick a basket of wild berries for Mama Squatch. She was planning to make one of her famous pies. The Squatch got up with the sunrise and began to make his way through the forest, out to the berry bush patch.

8

He crossed through the winding river, down the old dusty logging road, and under the splashing waterfall. Soon, he came to his favorite spot in the whole forest: the lookout.

The lookout was a place where the trees parted and the ground stopped sharply. The view showed nearly the entire forest below; there were tree tops as far as the eye could see.

The Squatch slowed his walk as he passed the lookout. He wanted to stay and gaze, but he had a pie to prepare for!

When he finally reached the berry patch, the bright sun felt warm on his face. The berries were plump and ripe for picking. The Squatch got right to work and his basket was filled in no time!

When his basket could not hold another berry, he picked a few more for himself and started back to his cave.

He reached the lookout again, and this time he decided to reward himself with a short rest. He sat on a large rock, enjoying the view, and some of his juicy berries.

After a few minutes, the Squatch began hearing an unfamiliar sound. It was coming from just over the ridge. He acted quickly and hid behind a large Oak tree. He waited, and watched, and listened as the noise grew louder.

And then he saw something his eyes could not believe…

HUMANS!

There were 3 of them! And boy, did they look... **DIFFERENT!**

The humans walked right past his hiding spot without seeing him. They stopped and put their packs down at the lookout.

The Squatch watched the humans safely from behind the tree.
He wanted to make a run for his cave, but it was too far.

He decided to sit and wait for them to leave.
The Squatch continued to watch and listen as the
humans talked. He did not move a muscle.

NEVER EVER
NO NO NO

As he sat, he remembered the stories his
parents told him: Squatch and humans
do not mix!

But from behind the tree, he saw the humans laughing and smiling. They did not seem mean, or one bit dangerous. They actually looked friendly, he thought.

After a while, he no longer felt scared. He even wanted to meet them.

The Squatch gathered **ALL** of his courage and took a **DEEP** breath. He started walking toward the humans to say "Hello".

He was so nervous his underarm fur was damp!

Just then, one of the young humans got too close to the ledge and started to lose her balance…

But the Squatch acted fast!
He dashed toward the edge
of the lookout!

He made it just in time! With help from the others, the Squatch pulled the young human back to safety!

The humans were so grateful; they all hugged the Squatch tightly. They were not scared of him; not one bit!

22

Soon, they realized they were not so different after all! The humans and the Squatch talked for hours. They each had so many questions.

As the sun began to sink in the sky, the new friends said their 'Goodbyes'. The humans promised to come visit the Squatch again, soon.

Or maybe, just maybe, the Squatch would
make the trip down to the big city...

The End.